The NOISY CLASSROOM

Written by Angela Shanté

Illustrated by Alison Hawkins

WEST
MARGIN
PRESS

In my school, Ms. Johnson teaches third grade.

This is the noisy class.

The door is always closed, but when I go to the bathroom, I hear music wafting into the hallway.

Music in school? The absurdity.

In my classroom we sit in orderly columns and rows, and only speak when called on.

Ms. Johnson's students chatter all day and loudly tumble into the hall.

In my class we walk in two silent lines.

Every day after school, parents wait impatiently outside Ms. Johnson's class, even though school lets out at 3 p.m.

Who would want to spend one extra minute in school?

And Ms. Johnson is noisy too.

She likes to sing. Loud.
And she is always dancing.
I think she is very odd.

I am going to third grade next year. Any class but the noisy class will do.

When I find out I will be going to Ms. Johnson's class, I tell my parents I am never, ever, going back to school.

I tell them I will get a job and move to Antarctica.

They speak in worried, hushed voices when they think I am not listening.

That summer they make my favorite foods
for every Sunday dinner. But empanadas
and jerk chicken will not make me budge.

All summer I worry.

All summer I pack for
my move to Antarctica.

"You don't know... it might be fun," Pa says.

"I can have fun in Antarctica," I mumble.

Ma says, "You will be in the class with Maia." But I think... *Maia and I can move to Antarctica together.*

Soon it is September. I trudge up the stairs to room 308.

Nervous third graders line up in the hallway. I wave to some of my friends in line and one warily waves back.

They look like they would rather be in Antarctica too.

I try to make one last plea to my parents, but they smile and give me four thumbs up.

We wait. And wait...

At 8 a.m. the door to room 308 swings open.
Ms. Johnson belts out, "Good morning!" I walk
into the classroom and swallow a cry when
she closes the door behind us. *I will move to
Antarctica tomorrow,* I promise myself.

This class looks weird. There are only a few chairs, some balls, a wobbly two-legged stool, and a huge floor rug. *Where is everyone supposed to sit?*

Ms. Johnson says, "Find a comfortable spot."

Anywhere? This is chaos, I think.

I sit on the rug next to Colin and Maia. We look uneasily at one another. *We could all move to Antarctica together.*

3ᴿᴰ GRADE

MS. Johnson

Ms. Johnson says, "Every day will begin with morning class meetings, and we'll always end the day cleaning up. A clean house is a happy mouse!"

I think that is odd. A mouse would probably be happier living in a dirty house. But that isn't even the weirdest part of the day.

Every lesson seems like a game. I have to admit, it is really fun.

But I keep thinking, *Are we going to learn anything today?*

When we play math-ball, I know how to skip-count by threes and make three shots for my team.

After lunch, we pretend to be ants and write stories from our tiny point of view.

The day passes by in a blur. I don't remember learning one single thing. Before I know it, it is 3:01 p.m., and we just finish tidying up the classroom.

When Ms. Johnson opens the door, she apologizes for keeping us late. She sings each student out in a robot voice. This makes the parents and students laugh.

That night at dinner my parents want to know all the details. The good. The bad. And the odd.

I try not to sound too thrilled when I tell them about the poem Ms. Johnson read by Nikki Giovanni. I tell them that we played all day and didn't learn a single thing. Ma got that worried crinkle between her eyebrows.

I tell them that I am still considering Antarctica, and Pa shoots Ma a look as he passes the plantains.

The rest of the week whizzes by.

We play math-ball, write calculations on our desk with dry erase markers, and freeze-dance all the way to lunch. As you can imagine, we are quite noisy.

FREEZE!

On Friday I notice a line of second graders at the water fountain. They quietly stand in two neat rows.

I wait my turn in the back. Under my breath I sing the clean-up song Ms. Johnson taught us, and the kids look at me suspiciously. I hear one of them call me odd.

When I open the classroom door, the clean-up song wafts into the hall. Ms. Johnson is singing and doing a shoulder shimmy. I turn around to the second graders and think... *My noisy class is way better than Antarctica.*

To my past, current, and future students; the world is in your hands. —A.S.

Edited by Clarissa Wong

Library of Congress Cataloging-in-Publication Data

Names: Shanté, Angela, author. | Hawkins, Alison, illustrator.
Title: The noisy classroom / written by Angela Shanté ; illustrated by Alison Hawkins.
Description: [Berkeley : West Margin Press, 2020] | Audience: Ages 6–8. | Audience: Grades 2–3. | Summary: "A young girl worries about entering the third grade because she's put into the noisy classroom, but she learns that school can be both fun and educational in nontraditional classes"— Provided by publisher.
Identifiers: LCCN 2019045148 (print) | LCCN 2019045149 (ebook) | ISBN 9781513262925 (hardback) | ISBN 9781513262932 (ebook)
Subjects: CYAC: Schools—Fiction. | Teachers—Fiction. | Worry—Fiction.
Classification: LCC PZ74832 Noi 2020 (print) | LCC PZ74832 (ebook) | DDC [E]—dc23
LC record available at https://lccn.loc.gov/2019045148
LC ebook record available at https://lccn.loc.gov/2019045149

Proudly distributed by Ingram Publisher Services

Printed in China
24 23 22 21 20   1 2 3 4 5

Published by West Margin Press

WEST MARGIN PRESS

WestMarginPress.com

WEST MARGIN PRESS
Publishing Director: Jennifer Newens
Marketing Manager: Angela Zbornik
Editor: Olivia Ngai
Design & Production: Rachel Lopez Metzger